THE Berenstain BEAR SCOUTS
and the
Magic Crystal Caper

Look for more books in
The Berenstain Bear Scouts series:

*The Berenstain Bear Scouts
in Giant Bat Cave*

*The Berenstain Bear Scouts
and the Humongous Pumpkin*

*The Berenstain Bear Scouts
Meet Bigpaw*

*The Berenstain Bear Scouts
Save That Backscratcher*

*The Berenstain Bear Scouts
and the Terrible Talking Termite*

*The Berenstain Bear Scouts and the
Coughing Catfish*

*The Berenstain Bear Scouts and the
Sci-Fi Pizza*

*The Berenstain Bear Scouts
Ghost Versus Ghost*

*The Berenstain Bear Scouts
and the Sinister Smoke Ring*

THE Berenstain BEAR SCOUTS
and the
Magic Crystal Caper

by Stan & Jan Berenstain
Illustrated by Michael Berenstain

A
LITTLE APPLE

SCHOLASTIC INC.
New York Toronto London Auckland Sydney

No part of this publication may be reproduced in whole or in part, or stored in a retrieval system, or transmitted in any form or by any means, electronic, mechanical, photocopying, recording, or otherwise, without written permission of the publisher. For information regarding permission, write to Scholastic Inc., 555 Broadway, New York, NY 10012.

ISBN 0-590-94475-4

Copyright © 1997 by Berenstain Enterprises, Inc.
All rights reserved. Published by Scholastic Inc.
APPLE PAPERBACKS and the APPLE PAPERBACKS logo are trademarks and/or registered trademarks of Scholastic Inc.

12 11 10 9 8 7 6 5 4 3 2 1   7 8 9/9 0 1 2/0

Printed in the U.S.A.

First Scholastic printing, June 1997

• Table of Contents •

1. The Beginning of a Strange Adventure   1

2. "Let's Tell Gramps"   9

3. The Great Gran: Knows All, Sees All   18

4. The Odd Couple   22

5. Big News!   32

6. A Pink Glow   39

7. Big Trouble at Beartown Lanes   45

8. Pay Up, or Else!   53

9. Pin Boys (and Girls) to the Rescue   60

10. A Star Is Born   68

11. I've Gotta Have It!   75

12. In the Dark of Night   80

13. Three Bags Full   82

14. The Morning After the Night Before   85

15. A Lovely Time Was Had by All   94

and the
Magic Crystal Caper

• Chapter 1 •

The Beginning of a Strange Adventure

If someone were to tell you that the Bear Scouts would have an adventure that included desperate danger from crashing objects the size of cannonballs, the Beartown June Fete, atomic energy, and a magic crystal ball, you might say, "Hey, wait a minute." Well, the answer to that is, "Hey, *you* wait a minute." Because that's just what happened. If you want to know the who, what, when, and why of *how* it happened, just keep reading.

It all started on a Saturday morning in June.

"What do you suppose she wants to see us about?" said Sister.

"Dunno," said Brother.

"No idea," said Fred.

Lizzy didn't answer. She was too busy talking to a tiny cabbage butterfly that had lit on her finger. That's the way it was with Lizzy. She often talked to butterflies and other like creatures. What's more, they seemed to listen.

The troop was on Scout Leader Jane's doorstep, waiting for her to answer the bell.

"Maybe you'd better ring again," suggested Fred.

Brother was about to, when the door flew open and there stood Jane. She looked like someone who had wonderful news and could hardly wait to tell it. "Good morning, scouts. This way, please."

The scouts followed Jane into the kitchen, where the table was set with five places. There was a glass of milk at each place and a big plate of raisin sugar cookies at the center. Raisin sugar cookies were Jane's specialty.

"Looks like a celebration," said Brother.

"Exactly," said Jane. "Sit, please."

"What are we celebrating?" asked Sister.

The scouts took their places, and the cookies were passed around. That first bite into one of Jane's raisin sugar cookies was something special. They were crunchy on the outside, soft on the inside, covered all over with fat raisins, and still warm from the oven. The second, third, and fourth bites weren't bad, either.

"Have you ever heard of the Supertroop Merit Badge Award?" asked Jane.

"I think so," said Brother. "But I'm not sure what it is."

"Well," said Jane. "It's just the biggest, most important honor a Bear Scout troop can receive. And guess what? I've put you up for it."

"Put us up for it?" said Fred. The scouts looked puzzled.

Jane picked up a folder that was beside her plate. It was filled with papers. "The Supertroop Merit Badge," she said, "isn't like the regular merit badges you've earned: the rock-climbing badge, the environmental badge, and others. It's a special badge awarded to . . . but let me read what it says in the *Official Bear Scout Handbook*."

Jane got up and left the kitchen. The scouts were still looking puzzled when she returned. She opened the handbook and started to read.

" 'The Supertroop Merit Badge Award is the highest honor in the annals of scoutdom. It is awarded to one Bear Scout troop each year by the Bear Scout High Council for achieving the following:

1. Living up to the highest standard of the Bear Scout Oath.

2. Earning five or more Bear Scout merit badges.

3. Serving the community above and beyond the call of Bear Scout duty.'

"There's lots more," continued Jane. "But it all boils down to this: I've put your troop's record together in this folder. Today I'm sending it along to the Bear Scout High Council in Big Bear City."

"Wow!" said Brother.

"How about that!" said Sister.

"Golly!" said Fred.

"Totally awesome!" said Lizzy.

"Hundreds of troops are submitted for the Supertroop Merit Badge Award each year," said Jane. "It's a very high honor indeed. Here's what it looks like." Jane held

the guidebook open to a picture of the
award.

The scouts were impressed. The award
looked almost like one of those fancy belts
boxers receive when they become champions. It made all those other badges look

like something you'd get in a cereal box. The scouts thought how great it would look on display in their secret chicken coop clubhouse at the far edge of Farmer Ben's farm. It might even impress the chickens who sometimes wandered in by mistake.

"When will the high council make its decision?" asked Brother.

"By the end of the month," said Jane.

"What do you think they'll decide?" asked Sister.

"How should I know?" said Scout Leader Jane with a hearty laugh. "I don't have a crystal ball."

• Chapter 2 •

"Let's Tell Gramps"

There was no question about it. Getting put up for the Supertroop Merit Badge Award was a high honor. The Bear Scouts were filled with pride as they left Scout Leader Jane's.

"I know what," said Sister. "Let's tell Gramps."

"Good idea," said Brother.

Though Jane was their Scout Leader — and a very good one she was — it was Gramps who was their friend and advisor. Not only was Gramps always there when he was needed, he was always in the same place — on Saturday mornings, at least. Saturday was Gramps's morning for sitting on his regular bench in the town square.

As the scouts headed for the town square, they pictured Gramps sitting on his bench reading his paper in the shade of Old Shag, the great historic tree (and backscratcher) that he and the scouts had saved from the chainsaw and the schemes of Mayor Honeypot and his crooked friend

WASHINGTON BEAR

Ralph Ripoff. And speaking of the Devil, wasn't that Ralph cutting across the square and heading up Main Street? And hadn't Chief Bruno warned Ralph to keep his crooked tricks and schemes out of town?

The scouts tried to keep an eye on Ralph when possible. But he didn't seem to be up to any mischief at the moment. Besides, they were on a mission to tell Gramps about the Supertroop Merit Badge Award.

But when they reached the town square, Gramps wasn't there. The scouts wondered why.

"Do you think there's something wrong?" said Sister.

"I doubt it," said Brother. "Something just came up, that's all."

"I mean there's no law that says he's got to be here *every* Saturday morning," said Fred.

Despite what they were saying, the scouts couldn't help being a little worried.

"Hey," said Lizzy. "Let's zip over to Gramps and Gran's and check up on him just to be sure."

The scouts headed up Main Street at a

good pace. The route to Gramps and Gran's was up Main Street and over Ridge Road. It wasn't long before they saw Ralph, dead ahead. He was walking along, tipping his hat to ladies, stopping to pass the time of day with this or that group of his fellow bears. Ralph didn't seem to be doing anything suspicious, but the scouts decided to investigate anyway.

They edged closer, and when Ralph stopped to exchange the time of day with a group of bears standing in front of Biff Bruin's Pharmacy, the scouts slipped into the alleyway and watched. It quickly became clear that Ralph wasn't exchanging the time of day. What was being exchanged was money. As the money changed hands, Ralph wrote things down in a little black book.

"Well, I'll be!" whispered Brother. "He's making book!"

"Making book?" whispered Sister.

"Taking bets," said Brother.

"I don't understand," said Lizzy.

"You will. Just watch. YO, RALPH!" he shouted.

The effect was something to see. Money and bears flew in all directions. Except for Ralph, who was on his knees picking up money.

"What are you doing, Ralph?" said Brother. "Taking orders for goldbricks?"

"Gracious, no," said Ralph. "I haven't engaged in the dishonest practice of selling goldbricks for years. Haven't you heard?" He continued getting up and brushing off the knees of his snazzy green suit. "I'm a legitimate businessbear now. In fact, I expect folks to start calling me 'Honest Ralph Ripoff' any minute."

"But, Ralph! You're taking bets," said Brother. "Do you call that legitimate?"

"Oh," said Ralph. "It may be a shade illegal. But it's honest. I'm just providing a service to those who wish to predict the future: the score of a baseball game, the results of an election, the price of honey. I keep careful records." He held up the black book. "I pay off promptly on all bets. I keep a small profit to hold body and soul together and to buy crackers and cuttle-bones for my friend Squawk. As I said, friends, I'm a legitimate businessbear."

Squawk was Ralph's pet parrot. They lived together on a broken-down old houseboat that was moored in a smelly backwater of Great Roaring River.

"Suppose Chief Bruno catches you," said Sister.

"That might be a problem," said Ralph. "Except that I happen to know that the chief and Officer Marguerite often have a friendly game of cards at the station on slow nights. And what about the bingo game they run at the town hall every

Tuesday? Well, I have some wagers to pay off. So, if you'll excuse me. Ta-ta."

That's the way it was with Ralph. He was as smooth as silk and twice as strong in the tug-of-war between right and wrong.

But the scouts had reached Ridge Road. It was time to cut over and check up on Gramps.

• Chapter 3 •

The Great Gran: Knows All, Sees All

The scouts' plan was to cut across the empty lot next to the hospital. That would be the quickest way to Gramps and Gran's. But they couldn't, because there was a fence around the lot and it wasn't empty anymore. Crews of workbears were setting things up for the June Fete.

The June Fete was a big Beartown event. It was put on every year to raise money for the hospital. It usually had a flower show, an antique sale, a food court, an art exhibition — all sorts of spring things. But the spring thing that caught Brother's attention was a small booth that was being put up. It had a sign on it. The sign said "The Great Gran: Knows All, Sees All."

"Hey," said Brother, stopping in his tracks. "We can kill two birds with one stone! Remember when Scout Leader Jane said —"

"I wish you wouldn't say that," said Lizzy.

"Say what?" said Brother.

"That thing about killing two birds with one stone," said Lizzy.

"But, Lizzy," said Brother. "It's just an expression."

"It may be just an expression," said Lizzy. "But it's brutal and ugly, and I wish you wouldn't say it."

Brother sighed. Scout Lizzy was so into nature's creatures that she wouldn't even swat a mosquito. But that's what made the "one for all and all for one!" Bear Scouts such a great team. Each member brought something special to the troop. Brother was a natural leader. Sister was all nerve. Fred was all brains, and Lizzy . . . well, Lizzy was just Lizzy.

"As I was saying," said Brother, choosing his words carefully, "I think we can accomplish two goals at the same time. Remember when Scout Leader Jane said, 'How would I know what the council will decide? I don't have a crystal ball'?"

The scouts remembered.

"Well, don't you get it?" said Brother. "We know somebody who *does* have a crystal ball. *Gran has one!* She tells fortunes every year at the June Fete. Goal one: We check up on Gramps. Goal two: We get Gran to look into her crystal and see whether we're going to get the Supertroop Merit Badge Award. Come on!"

Fred was about to protest. To his mind, the idea of predicting the future by looking into a crystal ball was not only unscientific, it was downright silly. But, then again, he couldn't see any harm in it. He hurried to catch up with the rest of the troop.

• Chapter 4 •

The Odd Couple

Gramps and Gran's house was just up ahead. The scouts could see Gran working in her garden. That was a relief. Gran wouldn't be out front calmly planting petunias if Gramps weren't all right.

"Hi, Gran!" called Brother. The rest of the troop echoed Brother's greeting. Gran looked up from her work and waved.

Gramps and Gran were an interesting couple. While Gramps was a terrific person, he could be a bit difficult. He had strong opinions on just about everything and was ready to argue about them at the

drop of a hat — as often as not with
Gran. Gran, on the other hand, was a
kind, friendly person with a ready smile.
And while they were a loving couple, they
had very different interests.

HI, GRAN!

Gramps was into fishing, building ships in a bottle, carving monkeys out of peach pits, complaining about the government. And, of course, there was his lifelong passion: bowling. Gramps had bowled since he was a cub, and loved it dearly. So much so, he would sometimes call up Beartown Lanes, get Billy the manager on the phone and say, "Billy, just let me hear those pins

drop." Then he would listen to the rolling thunder of the bowling balls and the crash and clatter of the falling pins for a while. It was music to his ears.

Gramps and bowling went back a long way. His first job as a youngster was as a pin boy. That was way back before they had automatic pinspotters to set up the pins after each bowl.

Gran's interests lay in the direction of gardening, quilt-making, cookery, and her lifelong passion: fortune-telling. Gran would read anything from tea leaves, palms, and coffee grounds to fireplace ashes and dust devils under the bed.

One of the things Gramps had a strong opinion on was Gran's fortune-telling. The idea that you could predict the future by staring into a glass ball struck Gramps as just about the dumbest, time-wastingest thing he could think of.

It happened that Gran had a similar opinion about Gramps's bowling habit. She thought the idea of grown bears spending their lives knocking over poor defenseless tenpins was utterly silly.

"Well, what do you think of my petunias?" said Gran as she stood up and brushed herself off.

"They're beautiful, Gran," said Sister.

"I can't decide whether to exhibit my

petunias or my hollyhocks at the June Fete," she said. "The hollyhocks are those tall fellows over there."

"They're both nice," said Brother. "Say, Gran, is Gramps around? There's something we want to tell him."

"Is it a secret?" said Gran.

"Goodness, no," said Lizzy.

"It's just that our troop has been put up for the Supertroop Merit Badge Award," said Fred. "It's a high honor, and we wanted to tell him about it."

"It sounds like a high honor," said Gran. "I'm sure he'll want to hear about it. But he's not here right now."

"Oh?" said Brother.

"He's over at Beartown Lanes," said Gran.

"Beartown Lanes?" said Fred.

"But Gramps never goes bowling on Saturday mornings," said Brother.

"Oh, he's not bowling. Didn't even take

his bowling ball," said Gran. "Come up on the porch and sit a while. I want to rest my bones."

The scouts followed Gran onto the wide front porch, which was lined with rockers.

"I don't know what he's doing over there," Gran went on. "He's been acting strangely all morning. He'd get on the phone, then he'd sit at his desk and scribble in a notebook. Then he'd jump up and walk around in circles talking to himself. Then he said, 'Got to go over to the bowling alley!' Jumped into his pickup and *vroom-vroom,* off he went. Well, you know how Gramps is about bowling. But I want to hear more about this special merit badge you've won."

"Oh, we haven't won it yet, Gran," explained Brother. "In fact, one of the reasons we came over was to ask you to look in your crystal ball and maybe see if we're *going* to win."

"Happy to. But can't right now," said Gran. "Because it just so happens that my crystal ball is over at the bowling alley, too."

"Huh?" chorused the scouts.

"Oh, it's not so strange as all that," explained Gran. "My crystal ball is heavy and awkward to handle. Especially with the June Fete coming up and all. So I got the idea of having it drilled with finger holes. You know, like a bowling ball. Figured I oughta be able to get *some* good out of Gramps's bowling habit. But I'll be glad to give you a reading when I get my crystal back."

"That'll be great, Gran," said Brother. "And would you tell Gramps how we're up for the Supertroop Merit Badge Award?"

"You can tell him yourself," said Gran. "Here comes Old Vroom-Vroom now."

• Chapter 5 •

Big News!

Gramps pulled into the driveway and climbed out of the pickup carrying a blue plaid bowling bag. But Gran said he hadn't taken his ball with him.

"Hello, scouts!" cried Gramps. "Glad you're here! I've got great news."

"We've got great news, too," said
Brother. "Scout Leader Jane's put us up
for the Supertroop Merit Badge Award."

"We were hoping to have Gran look into
her crystal," said Sister. "But she says it's
over at the bowling alley."

"Not anymore it isn't," said Gramps.
"It's right here in this bowling bag, all
drilled and proper. Come on into the
house."

Gran and the scouts followed him in.
"I'm glad to have my crystal back," said
Gran. "But where did that beautiful blue
plaid bowling bag come from? It's exactly
like yours."

"From the bowling alley's equipment counter," said Gramps. "It's a gift. They threw it into the deal."

"What deal?" said Gran.

"That's my big news," said Gramps. *I bought the bowling alley!*"

The news hit Gran like a shock wave. "You . . . you bought the bowling alley?" she said, choking on each word.

"That's right!" said Gramps. "It took all our life savings. But it was the chance of a lifetime."

"You can't be serious!" gasped Gran.

"Smartest thing I ever did!" said Gramps. "Beartown Lanes is a going business. It's a gold mine. Throws off cash like a money machine. And just think, I'll be able to bowl for free anytime I want."

"Who'd you buy it from?" asked Gran.

"Squire Grizzly, of course," said Gramps.

"Well, if it's such a going business,

why did the squire want to sell it?" asked
Gran.

"Good grief, woman," said Gramps.
"Don't you understand business? Squire
Grizzly owns half of Bear Country. What's
he need with a little old bowling alley?
Beartown Lanes is chicken feed to him."

"It may be chicken feed to the squire,"
said Gran. "But it's our life savings to us."
Gran sighed. "Oh, well. What's done is
done. Scouts, why don't I have a look into
my crystal and see about that Supertroop
Merit Badge Award?"

"We'll sure appreciate it," said Sister.

Gran unzipped the blue plaid bowling
bag and carefully lifted the heavy crystal
out of the bag. After checking to see if the
new finger holes were a good fit, she
placed it on the small round table she
used for home readings. The scouts gath-
ered round as Gran stared into the crystal
and began to say her magic words:

"Grizzly growl, grizzly grum,
tell me, crystal,
what is to come.
Tell us the future.
Help us see.
What will the council's
decision be?"

Gran stared hard into the crystal.

"What do you see, Gran?" said Brother. The rest of the troop chimed in.

"Nothing. It's all foggy," said Gran after a long pause.

"Maybe the finger holes messed it up," said Sister.

Gran sighed. "No, it's not the crystal," she said. "It's me. I can't concentrate. I'm just too upset about Gramps putting our life savings into a *bowling alley*."

The scouts could see Gramps was in for it for what he'd done. But when Gran wheeled around to face him, she accidentally knocked the crystal ball off the table. It hit the floor with a huge KLUNK!

"My crystal! My precious crystal!" cried Gran as it rolled across the floor.

• Chapter 6 •

A Pink Glow

Gran was right to worry about her crystal. It was rolling toward the steps that led to the sunken living room. The steps were stone, there were four of them, and they led to the sunken living room's stone floor.

There were four sickening glassy thuds as the crystal bounced down the steps. The scouts ran to the steps. They hovered over the crystal.

"I'm afraid to ask," cried Gran. "Is it smashed to bits?"

"No," said Brother. "It isn't even cracked."

"But there's *something* wrong with it,"
said Fred. "It's got a sort of pink glow inside it."

"A pink glow?" said Gramps. "Lemme
have a look."

"Just bring it here!" said Gran.

Fred picked it up and started to carry it to Gran. But he didn't get very far. "YOW! IT'S HOT!" he cried, tossing it into the air.

For the next seconds the Bear Scouts played hot potato with Gran's glowing crystal. It would have crashed to the floor again if Gramps hadn't come to the rescue and caught it in his big strong hands.

"Hmm," he said. "It seems to have cooled off some. It's still plenty warm, though. And I'll be danged. It does have a pink glow inside."

"Weird with a capital 'W,'" said Brother.

"What do you make of it, Fred?" said Lizzy. "You're our science guy."

"I don't know what to make of it," said Fred. "Unless smashing down those stone steps did something to the crystal's atomic structure."

"Is that possible?" asked Brother.

"Weird things happen sometimes," said Fred.

"Put it here on the table," said Gran. "I want to see this pink glow."

Gramps set the glowing crystal on the table. "Careful," he said. "It's still pretty warm."

Gran stared into the crystal. She started to say her magic words again. But she didn't even get to "grizzly grum." "It's clear!" she cried. "The fog is gone. I can see the future in the pink glow!"

The scouts got that crawly feeling you get when something really weird happens. And Gramps wasn't shaking his head anymore.

"Do you see anything about our Supertroop Merit Badge Award?" asked Brother.

"No," said Gran. "I see . . . I see . . . Beartown Lanes! It seems to be closed. There's a sign on the door. It says 'Closed Until Further Notice.'"

"Wait a minute! Let me see that!" said Gramps.

"The image has faded," said Gran. "Other images are coming into view. All sorts of images. Baseball scores: Yankees five, Giants three . . ."

"But that's tonight's game between the Big Bear City Yankees and the Beartown Giants," said Brother. "It hasn't even started yet!"

"I see a checkered flag," said Gran. "It's an auto race. The winning car is number six."

"That'll be the Grizzly Five Hundred," said Fred. "And it's not being run till next Tuesday!"

Gran fell back in her chair. She looked shaken up and exhausted.

"Are you all right, Gran?" said Sister.

"I saw the future," said Gran in a strange voice. *"I actually saw the future!"*

"Poppycock!" said Gramps. "Ridiculous!

There's no way Beartown Lanes is going out of business! Why, every lane is booked solid for two months. As for those scores and race results . . ."

That's when the phone rang. "Somebody answer that," said Gramps.

Brother picked up the phone. "Gramps and Gran's residence . . . it's for you, Gramps."

"The very idea of seeing the future in a glass ball," he mumbled as he picked up the phone. "Gramps here . . . yes . . . uh-huh . . ." All the strength seemed to go out of Gramps as he hung up the phone. "That was Billy the manager. Some sort of emergency over at the bowling alley. Gotta get over there right away."

GRAMPS HERE...
YES... UH —
HUH

• Chapter 7 •

Big Trouble at Beartown Lanes

"Easy, Gramps," said Brother. "Chief Bruno patrols this road. You don't want to get a ticket for speeding."

"Can't help that!" said Gramps as the pickup careened around a corner.

"Speeding *and* reckless driving," screamed Sister, hanging on for dear life. She and Brother were in the front of the truck with Gramps. Fred and Lizzy were hanging on for dear life in the back.

When Gramps got the emergency call from Billy the manager, he headed out the door with the scouts after him. They all piled into the pickup. Gramps broke all records getting to Beartown Lanes.

Jaws fell open with shock when they arrived. There on the door was exactly the same sign Gran had seen in her crystal ball. It said "Closed Until Further Notice." Gramps was especially shaken. Suppose, after all these years, it now turned out that Gran really *could* see the future.

Gramps tried the door. It was locked. He knocked hard.

"I guess you know what this means," said Brother. "It means that whatever strange atomic thing happened inside Gran's crystal when it fell down those steps, she really *can* see the future in it."

"That can't possibly be true," said Gramps. "And even if it is, I don't want to hear about it. Where *is* that Billy?"

Gramps banged on the door and shouted. "Billy! It's me, Gramps! Open up!"

"But suppose," said Fred, "the Yankees *do* beat the Giants five to three, and suppose number six *does* win the Grizzly Five Hundred. What then, Gramps?"

"I told you I didn't want to hear about it!" said Gramps. He was about to bang some more when the door opened and Billy peered out. Gramps and the scouts rushed in.

Once inside, Gramps looked around. When he had been there earlier and made his deal, Beartown Lanes had been a busy, noisy, bustling place. Bowling balls were thundering. Tenpins were crashing. The automatic pinspotters were setting up the pins as fast as the bowlers were knocking them down. Now the place was as silent and deserted as a tomb. But everything *seemed* in order. Why had Billy called? What had gone wrong?

"What's that funny smell?" said Brother, sniffing the air.

"I smell it, too," said Sister.

"It's a burnt smell," said Lizzy.

"Hmm," said Fred. "It smells like when my dad's computer went blooey."

"Yeah," said Gramps. "What *is* that smell? All right, Billy. What's going on? Why are we closed down?"

"Gee, it wasn't my fault, boss," said Billy.

"What wasn't your fault?" said Gramps.

"I mean, how was I supposed to know?" whimpered Billy.

"Billy," said Gramps. "If you don't tell what's going on, and right now, I'm going to use your mouth and nose for finger holes and roll *you* down the alley." He looked angry enough to do it, too.

"Okay! Okay!" said Billy. "Follow me."

Gramps and the scouts followed him across the lanes and down a passageway to the rear of the building.

"There's the problem," said Billy. He was pointing to a big flat black box that was attached to the wall. It was giving off a strong burnt smell, and there were scorch marks on the wall.

"What is this thing?" said Gramps.

Billy didn't seem to want to answer. But when Billy saw Gramps flexing his big bony fists, he started talking fast. "It's the master computer that runs the automatic pinspotter. It's finished, completely burnt out. You can't operate Beartown Lanes without it. It's been on its last legs for months. It'll cost thousands to replace. That's why Squire Grizzly sold you the place."

"Why, that no-good greedy crook!" said Gramps. "And you knew all about it, you little worm!" Gramps took hold of Billy's collar and bunched up a big fist.

"Easy, Gramps," cautioned Brother.

BELWOOD SCHOOL

"Socking Billy isn't going to solve anything."

"Brother's right," said Sister. "What
we've got to do is put our heads together
and get this place going again."

"I mean, you've got your life savings
sunk in this place," said Fred.

"Don't remind me," said Gramps.

"And," said Lizzy, "if you don't reopen
soon, you're going to lose all your cus-
tomers to McBruin's Bowlerama out on
the highway."

Gramps unbunched his fist and let go
of Billy's collar. "You're right, of course,"
said Gramps.

That's when somebody started banging
on the locked front door of Beartown
Lanes.

"Make yourself useful, Billy. Go see
what that banging's about."

• Chapter 8 •

Pay Up, or Else!

"This phony sign doesn't fool me for a minute! So open up and pay up!"

It was Ralph Ripoff, swindler, pickpocket, card shark, and, more recently, bookmaker, who was banging on the door of Beartown Lanes.

"You'd better open up, Billy! And I want my money!" Bang! Bang! Ralph hit air on his third bang. Billy had opened up.

"For Pete's sake, Ralph! That sign's not phony. And stop banging. The new owner's here, and the last thing I need is for him to know about my betting habit. Quick, let's slip into my office."

"New owner?" said Ralph.

"Yes. Gramps bought the place from Squire Grizzly."

"How come it's closed down?" said Ralph.

"Little problem with the automatic pinspotter," said Billy. "C'mon into my office."

Billy looked to make sure they hadn't been seen, then closed the door. It had been a rough day for him. First there was Gramps with his big bony fists, and now Ralph was demanding his money.

"Look," said Billy. "I know I owe you, and I'm going to pay."

"That's right," said Ralph, looking into his little black book. "You owe me big bucks, and you'd better pay up right now!"

"Gimme a break, Ralph," said Billy. "I just don't have the money right now. And

you know the old saying: 'You can't get blood out of a turnip.'"

"Well, I've got a new saying for you," said Ralph. "It goes like this: I know a couple of guys in Big Bear City that would enjoy getting some out of you."

Billy folded his arms and leaned against the wall of his tiny office. "Look, Ralph, I can't give you any money — at least not right now. But suppose I were to give you something that's worth thousands, even millions. Would you wipe out my debt?"

"What could you possibly give me that would be worth millions?" said Ralph.

"Information," said Billy. "Well, is it a deal?"

"Let's hear the information," said Ralph, sitting on the edge of Billy's desk.

"Well, it's like this," said Billy. "I knew there was going to be trouble when Gramps arrived, so I took my time opening the door. You know, so I could get my story straight. I heard talking outside. He had the scouts with him. It sounded interesting, so I listened."

"Get on with it, Billy," said Ralph. "I have other appointments."

"You know how Gran tells fortunes at the June Fete," continued Billy. "Sees the future in her crystal ball."

"You're wasting my time," said Ralph. "Gran couldn't predict getting wet in the rain. Now, if you'll excuse me, I've got to see a couple of guys about a turnip."

"No, Ralph! Wait!" cried Billy. "I'm just getting to the good part. It seems that something weird happened to Gran's crystal ball. It fell down some steps and turned atomic or something. It actually tells the future. It told about how the lanes would be closed down. It told the exact sign I put on the door."

"Oh?" said Ralph.

"But that's not all. It gave the score of

tonight's game between the Yankees and the Giants. The Yankees are going to win, five to three. And there's more. It told the winner of the Grizzly Five Hundred next Tuesday. Number six is going to win. Well, Ralph, is it a deal? Are we even?"

"Billy, you can't be serious," said Ralph. "You can't really expect me to cancel a large debt in exchange for a cockamamie story about an atomic crystal ball that tells baseball scores." Ralph tilted his straw hat to the proper angle and rose to leave. "But I'll tell you what I *will* do. I'll give you two more weeks to pay. Just because I like you. Well, ta-ta!"

"But, Ralph!" cried Billy, as Ralph left the office and slipped out the front door.

When last seen, he was walking away from Beartown Lanes, whistling, twirling his cane, and looking for all the world like the cat that swallowed the canary. Or maybe even the canary that swallowed the cat.

• Chapter 9 •

Pin Boys (and Girls) to the Rescue

"It's that danged crystal ball!" snarled Gramps. "I may just go home and smash it to bits."

"Now, Gramps," said Brother. "It's not Gran's crystal ball that's the problem. The problem is figuring out some way to get this place back in action."

Gramps and the scouts were sitting in one of the alcoves in front of the alleys where bowlers waited between turns. They were drinking sodas Gramps got from the lanes' refreshment counter.

"I know. I know," said Gramps. "I just can't help it. It was bad enough when Gran's fortune-telling was just for fun. But now that the dang crystal has gone atomic and she really can see the future . . . it's . . . it's . . . against nature! It's downright evil, by gosh!"

"Maybe not," said Fred. "Maybe it's some kind of scientific breakthrough. Maybe even a miracle."

"Yeah," said Sister. "Forget the Supertroop Merit Badge Award. Gran'll be able to predict anything — test scores, the weather, who's gonna win the Double-Dutch contest."

"I'll tell you one thing," said Lizzy. "When word gets out about Gran's new improved crystal ball, she's going to be the hit of the June Fete."

"Hey, that's right," agreed Brother. "Folks'll line up for miles to get their for-

tunes told. And speaking of fortunes, it's going to *make* one for the hospital."

"Yeah," said Gramps. "But how am I going to tell Gran I've lost ours in a dead bowling alley?"

"That's our point, Gramps. You won't have to if we can just figure out how to get this place up and going again."

But Gramps didn't seem to hear. He kept going on about Gran and her crystal. "It's evil, I tell you — and dangerous. Looking into the future and playing with people's lives like that . . ."

"Gramps," said Brother.

"Yes," said Gramps.

"Bowling goes back a long way, doesn't it?"

"A long way, indeed," said Fred, who read the encyclopedia for fun. "Bowling has been traced back hundreds of years. Originally called 'the game of bowls' . . ."

"Put a cork in it, Fred. I've got an idea," said Brother.

"Fred's right," said Gramps. "Bowling goes back a long way."

"What did they do before they had automatic pinspotters?" asked Brother.

"They had pin boys, of course," said Gramps. "And even some pin girls. Pin boy was my first job. That's how I met Gran.

We worked in the same bowling alley. You might say I fell in love with bowling and Gran at the same time."

"Exactly," said Brother.

"Exactly what?" said Gramps.

"That's how we'll reopen the bowling alley: with pin boys," said Brother.

"And pin girls," said Sister.

"Oh, I don't think that'll work," said Gramps. "I'm not as nimble as I used to be. I don't think my knees'll take it. As for Gran . . ."

"Not you and Gran!" said Brother.

"Then who?" asked Gramps.

"You're looking at us!" said Brother. "The Jack-be-nimble, Jack-be-quick, Jack-jump-over-the-bowling-balls Bear Scouts!"

"But it's dangerous," said Gramps. "You've got to be really nimble. Those bowling balls come at you like cannonballs. Those tenpins fly every which way."

"No problem," said Brother. "We're all

top soccer players. And Sister and Lizzy are Double-Dutch champions."

"I can even do red hot pepper," said Sister.

"Me, too," said Lizzy.

Gramps didn't exactly leap at the scouts' suggestion. But he was so eager to save Beartown Lanes that he decided to give it a try.

For the rest of the afternoon, bowling balls thundered and tenpins flew every

which way and the "Jack-be-nimble Bear Scouts" leaped about like mountain goats in an avalanche. Even Billy the manager was impressed. "You know, boss, with a few more cubs, I think this pin boy/pin girl thing can work. Why don't I put up some notices around town. You know, 'Pin boys and pin girls wanted at Beartown Lanes.' We've got clubs booked all day tomorrow."

"Do it, Billy," said Gramps. "It just might work. Maybe it can put us back in business long enough for me to get a loan for a new pinspotting system. But first get another round of sodas for me and my hardworking pinspotting crew."

"Sure thing, boss," said Billy.

The scouts were too short of breath to say their "one for all and all for one!" slogan. So they just crossed soda bottles and drank 'em down. Gramps joined them.

• Chapter 10 •

A Star Is Born

Lizzy had been right when she said that Gran would be the hit of the June Fete. At least that's how things were shaping up. It would have been hard to keep something as exciting as Gran's new improved crystal ball a secret, in any case.

But the June Fete Committee didn't even try. Quite the opposite. They called up the newspapers and TV stations. They arranged for newspaper stories and television appearances. Gran's picture was in the newspaper. It showed Gran looking into her crystal ball. The caption under the picture said "The Great Gran: Knows all, sees all." The television station did a news report about Gran. It showed her holding her blue plaid bowling bag.

Gran didn't tell the newspaper or television folk about her crystal's strange new power and warm pink glow. She kept that to herself. But warm pink glow or not, there was no question about it. Gran and her crystal ball had become the talk of the town.

And it was eating Gramps's heart out. The more talk there was about Gran and her crystal ball, the angrier and more upset he got. It was causing real trouble between Gramps and Gran. The scouts could see it happening, and it worried them. They loved them both, so, naturally, they didn't want to take sides.

Gramps was spending more and more time at Beartown Lanes tending to business, which was going pretty well. It turned out that lots of cubs wanted jobs as pin boys and pin girls. It was beginning to look like Gramps would be able to get a loan to buy a new automatic pinspotter.

But Gramps wasn't just tending to business. He had begun going to the bowling alley in the evenings as well. He just couldn't handle all the excitement and

fuss about Gran and her crystal ball.
When it got too much for him, he'd grab
his bowling bag, jump into his pickup, and
head for Beartown Lanes. Once there, he'd
unzip his bowling bag, lift out his black
marbleized bowling ball, sight down the
alley, and *let 'er rip!* It was almost as if
those pins were the June Fete Committee,

the newspaper reporters, the TV reporters, and maybe even Gran herself. Gramps got quite a few ten-strikes that way and worked off a lot of anger.

The scouts didn't really understand why Gramps was so angry about Gran's fortune-telling. They began to think that maybe, just maybe, he was jealous. They asked him about it at the bowling alley one day.

"Jealous? No, my friends," said Gramps. "Look, I've told you before why I'm against this whole fortune-telling business — especially her doing the June Fete thing. It was one thing when she was doing it just for fun. But now that she can really see the future, it's wrong! It's not only wrong, it's dangerous."

"But what's so wrong about it?" asked Brother.

"And why is it dangerous?" asked Sister.

"It's for a good cause," said Fred.

"It's going to raise money for the hospital," said Lizzy.

"That's all very well," said Gramps. "But look at it this way. Just think about all the folks who'll be lined up for readings at the June Fete. Suppose Gran looks into that creepy crystal of hers and sees that something awful is going to happen to somebody or somebody's loved ones. What is Gran supposed to do? Does she tell them the truth? Or does she lie and tell them that everything is going to be all right."

"I see what you mean, Gramps," said Brother.

"Yeah," said Sister. "It's kind of scary."

"Yeah," said Fred. "It's a great responsibility."

"I think Gramps is right," said Lizzy. "I think the future is nature's responsibility. I, for one, don't want to know the future.

After all, part of the fun of life is not knowing exactly what's going to happen next."

"Exactly!" said Gramps. "Look at what happened when the crystal said Beartown Lanes was finished. I gave up hope. I was ready to quit. But you weren't. You used the brains and spirit that nature gave you and saved the day."

"I see your point, Gramps," said Brother. "But what are you going to do?"

"I'm going to get her to cancel her 'Great Gran' act at the June Fete," said Gramps.

"That's not going to be easy," said Fred.

"Gran's a star now," said Sister. "And it's not easy to tell a star to stop shining."

Gramps sighed. "That's what's worrying me," he said.

• Chapter 11 •

I've Gotta Have It!

Ralph Ripoff was in the habit of pacing in circles when he had a really hard problem to solve. That's what he was doing now: pacing in circles in the grand salon of the run-down old houseboat where he lived with his pet parrot Squawk.

"Round he goes, round he goes!" squawked Squawk. "And where he stops —"

"Shut your beak!" commanded Ralph. "Can't you see I'm trying to think?"

"Trying to think. Trying to think," squawked Squawk.

"I've simply gotta have that crystal! It called both things right. The Yankees-Giants game and the Grizzly Five Hundred. And the six car was a hundred-to-one shot! Did you hear that, Squawk? A hundred to one!"

"Hundred to one. Hundred to one," squawked Squawk.

"Billy was right," said Ralph, continuing to pace. "That crystal ball would be worth millions to me. I could win every bet! I wouldn't want to, of course. I'd lose one every now and then to make things look good.

"I could steal it, of course. That would be easy. I could see where she keeps it in the newspaper picture, not to mention the TV news. But what good would that do? I'm the first one they come to when anything's missing."

"Guilty as charged. Guilty as charged," agreed Squawk.

"What I've got to do," said Ralph, sitting down in his easy chair, "is figure out
some way of stealing Gran's crystal *without anyone knowing it's missing!*"

He absentmindedly reached for the re-
mote control, turned on the TV, and began
channel surfing. TV shows flashed by —
*The Bear Stooges, B-Span, Bearwatch,
Lives of the Bear Rich and Famous, Bear
Trek.*

"Hold it!" cried Ralph, switching back
to *Lives of the Bear Rich and Famous.*

There on the TV screen was a place
that Ralph knew well. It was the magnifi-
cent mansion of Squire Grizzly, the richest
bear in Bear Country. The camera was
panning the squire's stately grounds.

"Of course!" cried Ralph, as the camera zoomed in on the beautiful birdbath that stood before the main entrance. It was lined with silvered glass. There was a small stand at its center and on the stand *a glass crystal!*

Ralph leaped up and hit himself on the side of the head. "Why didn't I think of it? I pass by there every day. And it's just the right size!"

"Right size. Right size," squawked Squawk.

• Chapter 12 •

In the Dark of Night

It was the wee hours of the day that would see the grand opening of the Beartown June Fete. A sliver of moon shone feebly on a dark form moving along the wall that was supposed to keep out the likes of night-crawler Ralph Ripoff. A low-hanging branch, and it was upsy-daisy over the wall and across the dewy grass and onto the entrance road. The birdbath of the rich and famous lay just ahead.

"Okay," said Ralph in a low voice. "Everybody out of the pool!"

Splashing night birds flew away as Ralph reached over and pried loose the garden crystal. He popped it into the blue plaid bowling bag he'd bought at Beartown Lanes. A quick zip of the zipper, and a quick zip back across the grass and over the wall and onto the road.

Next stop, the upstairs hall closet of Gramps and Gran's house on Ridge Road.

• Chapter 13 •

Three Bags Full

Prying the garden crystal loose from Squire Grizzly's birdbath had been the easy part. Exchanging it for Gran's crystal was going to be the hard part. The hall closet where Gran kept her crystal was on the second floor of the two-story house. Ralph was counting on his early experience as a second-story bear to help him make the exchange.

His skills came back to him as he felt his way along the side of the house. He came to a ladderlike trellis that led to an open upstairs window. After testing the trellis for strength, he hooked the handles of the bowling bag onto his arm and started to climb.

A quick look in the window revealed a bathroom in the soft glow of a plug-in night-light. A tight, awkward squeeze through the window, into and out of the bathroom, an *ever so careful* tiptoe along the hall — one chirp from a squeaky floorboard and all would be lost.

Groping his way along the hall, he felt the folding door of his destination, the hall closet where Gran kept her million-dollar crystal ball. A split-second flash of Ralph's penlight revealed Gran's bowling bag. He quickly exchanged his blue plaid bowling bag for hers, stole back along the hall, out the bathroom window, down the trellis, and headed happily for his houseboat home.

But there was just one problem. The quick flash of his penlight did not reveal that there was another identical blue plaid bowling bag in the hall closet. In other words, there were "three bags full."

The question was, full of what?

• Chapter 14 •

The Morning After
the Night Before

By the time the Bear Scouts reached Ridge Road, shouting could be heard a block away. Neighbors were looking out of their windows and shaking their heads. Squirrels peeped out of their hidey-holes and wondered what was going on. Nest-building robins stopped in their work and listened. What was going on, of course, was the biggest fight Gramps and Gran had ever had.

"Come on!" cried Brother. "It sounds pretty bad."

The scouts broke into a run.

But it was much worse than bad. The screaming and hollering were the least of it. The scouts rushed into the house to find Gramps trying to wrestle Gran's bowling bag away from her and Gran hanging onto it for dear life.

"Stop it, Gramps!" shouted Brother. "Stop it!"

The sound of Brother's voice and the sight of the Bear Scouts seemed to bring Gramps to his senses. He let go of Gran's bowling bag and looked at the scouts. Then he looked back at Gran and said, "You know what I'm going to do? I'm going bowling!" Then he picked up his blue plaid bowling bag, which had been sitting on Gran's little round table during the argument. Without another word he headed out the door.

Gran rushed to the door. She saw Gramps jumping into his pickup. "How am I going to get to the June Fete?" she cried.

"Take a taxi!" shouted Gramps. And off he roared.

"Don't worry, Gran," said Sister. "We'll see that you get to the June Fete in plenty of time."

"We'll call the committee," said Fred.

"Miserable old coot!" said Gran. "He's been angry as a bear ever since my crystal got its wonderful pink glow." She sat down in an armchair with the bowling bag in her lap. She unzipped it and reached in with both hands. "My beautiful, warm glowing crystal . . ."

Gran's eyes went wide as she lifted the crystal out of its bag. "This . . . this . . . ," she gasped, *"is not my crystal!"*

"Are you sure?" said Brother.

"Of course I'm sure!" said Gran. "This ball is cold! And this ball does not have a pink glow!"

"Maybe it's just lost its power," said Fred.

"Then," said Gran, holding up the crystal for all to see, "how do you explain the fact that it has no finger holes?"

It was a good question.

"It seems to me," said Brother, "that the explanation is that someone has exchanged your crystal for that glass ball."

"But why would anyone think they would get away with it?" said Gran.

"Because," said Brother, "whoever did it obviously didn't know your crystal has a warm glow and finger holes."

"But who would do such a terrible thing?" said Gran.

"How does our bookmaking friend Ralph sound as a candidate?" said Brother.

"Of course. He could win every bet with Gran's crystal," said Fred.

"But where did he get the exact same blue plaid bowling bag?" asked Lizzy.

"The same place Gramps and Gran got theirs: Beartown Lanes."

"That's it, then!" said Sister. "Ralph has Gran's crystal!"

"I don't think so," said Brother. "Put your hands on this table where Gramps's bowling bag was sitting, the way I'm doing."

Gran and the scouts put their hands on the table. "It's warm!" they chorused.

"What's it mean?" asked Gran.

"It means," said Brother, "that Ralph can't possibly be the one who has your crystal."

"Why not?" asked Gran.

"Because," said Brother, "it's Gramps who has it, and *he's just gone bowling with it!*"

"To the bowling alley!" cried Gran. "My precious crystal will be crashed to bits!" But that's not what happened.

Gran and the scouts were in luck when

they rushed out to flag a passing car. Chief Bruno happened to be driving by. They piled into the police car and, with siren screaming, they careened to Beartown Lanes.

But they were too late. Gramps was already into his backswing. He was much too angry to notice that his bowling ball was warm and had a strange pink glow. Going into his powerful three-step delivery, Gramps sent the atomic crystal down the alley for a perfect ten-strike.

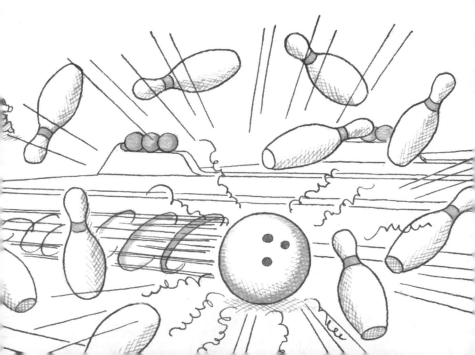

When the scouts reached the crystal at the end of the alley, it was cold and its pink glow was gone. Gran's crystal had lost its power.

Meanwhile, down by the river, in a run-down houseboat, Ralph was waking from a dream of untold millions. He climbed out of his bunk, zipped open the stolen bowling bag, and took out . . . *a bowling ball!*

"A bowling ball!" he screamed. "A no-good, worthless, crummy bowling ball!" Then, with a strength born of fury, he threw Gramps's heavy bowling ball through the salon window into the river.

"Set 'em up in the other alley! Set 'em up in the other alley!" squawked Squawk.

• Chapter 15 •

A Lovely Time Was Had by All

Gran took it all quite well. She admitted that the strange powers of her crystal ball were getting to be quite a responsibility.

The line at Gran's fortune-telling booth

was just as long as last year's. And folks seemed quite happy with Gran's readings. The scouts waited in line like everybody else. They still wanted to know about their chances for the Supertroop Merit Badge Award.

Gran looked deep into her crystal. She said her magic words.

"Sorry, scouts," she said. "I'm just not getting any feedback on that."

"That's okay, Gran," said Lizzy. "Because the way I look at it, half the fun of life is not knowing exactly what's going to happen next!"

• About the Authors •

Stan and Jan Berenstain have been writing and illustrating books about bears for more than thirty years. Their very first book about the Bear Scout characters was published in 1967. Through the years the Bear Scouts have done their best to defend the weak, catch the crooked, joust against the unjust, and rally against rottenness of all kinds. In fact, the scouts have done such a great job of living up to the Bear Scout Oath, the authors say, that "they deserve a series of their own."

Stan and Jan Berenstain live in Bucks County, Pennsylvania. They have two sons, Michael and Leo, and four grandchildren. Michael is an artist, and Leo is a writer. Michael did the pictures in this book.

Don't Miss

THE Berenstain BEAR SCOUTS

**and the
Run-Amuck Robot**

"Look!" hissed Fred.

"I see! I see!" hissed Brother in return.

"What's that clicking noise?" whispered Sister.

"It's — it's — it's my t-t-teeth chattering," said Lizzy.

The professor turned a dial. The crackling got louder. The huge coil began to glow.

"It's just like that old book," said Fred. "The one about Dr. Frankenbear."

"Not now, Fred," said Brother.

"You know," said Fred. "He was the one

who wanted to create life. He tried to make a person out of parts of dead bears."

"Please, Fred," said Sister.

"Only it turned out to be a monster with a bolt through its neck," said Fred.

"We know, we know," said Lizzy.

"And he did it with electricity!" said Fred.

The crackling sound was now continuous. The coil glowed red. The stench of ozone filled the air. Gus had begun cranking the handle of the static electricity machine. Now he was cranking it faster and faster. The scouts could feel the electricity in their fur.

The professor gave the big dial another turn. A pale blue tongue of electricity reached out of the glowing coil. Then another turn, and the blue tongue *ZAPPED* the body beneath the cloth!

Nothing happened. The body beneath the cloth lay perfectly still.

"Thank goodness!" whispered Brother. "Whatever he was trying to do, it didn't work. Come on. Let's get out of here while the getting's good."

The scouts began inching back along the ledge. They simply had to escape from this awful place. But there was some kind of ruckus going on down below. Gus and the professor were arguing. Actual Factual was reaching for the master switch. Gus was trying to stop him.

"No, Professor! No!" cried Gus. "You'll fry us all!"

But the professor wouldn't be stopped. He reached up and threw the master switch!

The room went white with a blinding light. Jagged bolts of lightning split the air. *ZAP! ZAP! ZAP!*

And there before the Bear Scouts' very eyes, the body beneath the cloth sat up.